FAME SCHOOL

Glamour! Talent! Stardom! Fame and fortune could be one step away for the kids of Fame School! All the students at Rockley Park, a school for the pop culture performing arts, are talented, but they still have to work hard. They must keep up their grades, learn about the professional side of the music business, improve their talent, *and* get along with their classmates. Being a star—and a kid—isn't easy. Things don't always go as planned, but one thing's certain—this group of friends will do their best to sing, dance, and jam their way to the top!

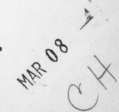

Tara's Big Plan

"What are you doing?" Chloe asked Tara.

"I looked up Tikki Deacon's charity on the Internet," Tara told her. "And it's all here. The school where they did the fashion shoot can only take care of fifty children, and according to this there are *thousands* who need the same help, but there just isn't the money to do it. And that school *does* need more money urgently or it might have to close."

"That's terrible," said Chloe. "It won't close now, though, with Tikki Deacon helping, will it?"

"I don't know," Tara told her. "In my experience, adults often let you down. Who knows? She might support them for a few weeks and then go on to something else. But the school needs help all the time." She thought for a moment and then turned to face Chloe. "When I see Mrs. Sharkey tomorrow, I'm going to ask if we can adopt the charity, and make it our job to help keep the school going."

"What an awesome idea!" said Chloe.

FAME SCHOOL

Tara's Triumph

CINDY JEFFERIES

PUFFIN BOOKS

For every child in need of help, wherever they may be.

Thanks to Ed for the loan of his bass
and Rickenbacker for making the beautiful 4003.

PUFFIN BOOKS
Published by the Penguin Group
Penguin Young Readers Group,
345 Hudson Street, New York, New York 10014, U.S.A.
Penguin Group (Canada), 90 Eglinton Avenue East, Suite 700, Toronto, Ontario,
Canada M4P 2Y3 (a division of Pearson Penguin Canada Inc.)
Penguin Books Ltd. 80 Strand, London WC2R 0RL, England
Penguin Ireland, 25 St Stephen's Green, Dublin 2, Ireland
(a division of Penguin Books Ltd)
Penguin Group (Australia), 250 Camberwell Road, Camberwell, Victoria 3124, Australia
(a division of Pearson Australia Group Pty Ltd)
Penguin Books India Pvt Ltd, 11 Community Centre, Panchsheel Park,
New Delhi - 110 017, India
Penguin Group (NZ), 67 Apollo Drive, Rosedale, North Shore 0745, Auckland, New Zealand
(a division of Pearson New Zealand Ltd.)
Penguin Books (South Africa) (Pty) Ltd, 24 Sturdee Avenue, Rosebank,
Johannesburg 2196, South Africa

Registered Offices: Penguin Books Ltd, 80 Strand, London WC2R 0RL, England

First published in Great Britain by Usborne Publishing Ltd., 2005
Published by Puffin Books, a division of Penguin Young Readers Group, 2007

1 3 5 7 9 10 8 6 4 2

Copyright © Cindy Jefferies, 2005
All rights reserved
CIP Data is available.

Puffin Books ISBN 978-0-14-240837-7

Printed in the United States of America

1. Alone

Tara stepped out of the shower and put on her last clean shirt. She looked longingly at her freshly made bed, with the mosquito netting neatly furled. But she couldn't go back to bed, even though she'd been up since five A.M., and had just returned from the morning's safari. She had a very long journey ahead of her and she wasn't looking forward to traveling alone.

She picked up her earphones and put some music on. She'd filled the player with all her favorite songs before she'd gone on vacation, and now she tried to blot out her tiredness with some heavy rock as she began to pack.

The staff at the game lodge had been kind to her.

The owners, Connie and Tambo Sissulu, were old friends of her parents. They had looked after Tara very well and had tried hard to make her feel at home. Jimmy, their safari guide, had been wonderful about including her, sometimes even letting her ride up in the front of the safari bus with him. But even seeing the "big five" game animals of Africa hadn't cheered Tara up. She was feeling very let down, and spending the last two days of her vacation with a variety of middle-aged couples, with their baggy shorts and tedious conversation, hadn't helped. She was sure none of them would share her passion for rock music, and she hadn't mentioned to anyone how much she missed playing her bass guitar.

It wasn't supposed to have been like this. It should have been a *family* vacation, a fantastic week on safari, all three of them together for once. But that's not how it had turned out. Things had gone wrong almost from the start.

"Unfortunately, I have to fly back home a couple of days early," Tara's dad had announced rather sheepishly over dinner on the first night. "I got a call this morning, asking me to step in at the last minute for a really important recording session. They need me in London on Friday."

"Oh no! Darling!" protested Tara's mom. "Can't you tell them you won't do it?"

"Sorry. No, I can't turn this one down," her father had replied. "But we'll still have five days on vacation together."

Tara had played with her exotic fruit salad while she listened to her parents' voices arguing against the night sounds of the African bush. *We should all be sitting quietly*, she thought, *listening to the fantastic roars and screeches out there in the dark*. But Tara's parents' careers got in the way of almost everything.

Tara's father was a jazz musician and her mother was a fashion journalist. They both spent lots of their time jetting around the world at a moment's notice, and now it seemed they couldn't even manage a week together as a family without one of them ruining everything.

Tara tried not to be too unhappy about her dad

having to leave early. But it turned out that her father wasn't going to be the only person to let her down. Her mother soon abandoned the family vacation as well.

After three wonderful days together, her mother had got wind of an important photo shoot happening on the coast. First there had been constant phone calls. Then she had dropped the bombshell.

"I have to leave in the morning, and won't be back for the rest of the week," she had announced, to Tara's dismay. "Don't be difficult, darling," she had added, noticing the look on Tara's face. "The rumor is that Tikki Deacon is in Africa for more than just a modeling assignment. You know how famous she is. It could be a really big story. I can't let my editor down, can I?"

So that was that. Three days as a family, two more with her dad, and the last two abandoned by *both* her parents. Tara bit back the angry words she felt like saying. Other people got to have real family vacations. Sometimes they spent as much as two whole weeks together. But the best her parents could manage was three days.

She listened while her parents discussed what they should do with their daughter for the final two days of the vacation, when they would both be away. Their conversation made Tara feel like a package.

"We could send her to my mother, but there's the problem of getting her back to school, now that Mother doesn't drive," Tara's mom mused.

"Do you have a friend you'd like to stay with, sweetie?" asked her dad hopefully. "That would make it easier to get her to school," he added to his wife, ignoring Tara's mumbled reply.

There wasn't anyone Tara wanted to stay with, especially at such short notice. She didn't want anyone feeling sorry for her. That would be too much to bear.

"Can't I fly back to London on Friday with you?" she had begged her dad.

But her father had been adamant. "As soon as I get back, I'll be in the studio, and you know what long hours that means," he told her. "I expect I'll be working through the night. That would be no fun for you, and I couldn't leave you at home for so long on your own either."

"Let's talk to Connie and Tambo," suggested her mom. "Just because *we* have to leave doesn't mean that Tara needs to miss the rest of the safari. I'm sure they'll be fine about keeping an eye on you," she told Tara cheerfully. "You wouldn't want to be dragged around with me in this heat, would you? You'll have lots to do here, with two game drives each day, and there's the pool to relax in, too."

"If we make sure she can connect directly to the London flight, she'll be fine," Tara's dad added to his wife. "And I'll arrange for a car to pick you up from Heathrow Airport and take you to school," he told Tara. And so that had been that.

Tara hadn't created a fuss, but soon afterward she made an excuse and went to her room. She put on some mellow music and stared miserably at her reflection in the dark window before she pulled the blinds. She wished she had her bass with her. At least music was reliable. It seemed it was the only thing in her life that was.

Once again, Tara would be showing up at school for

a new term without her mom and dad there to give her a hug and wish her well like all the other pupils. Rockley Park was a boarding school, and Tara hated arriving by herself. It just wasn't fair.

At least Tara enjoyed school. Although it offered all the usual classes, Rockley Park also taught the students everything they needed to know about making it in the music industry. And Tara had great musical ambitions. She dreamed of belonging to a famous rock band. She was determined to become more successful even than her dad. He was a well-respected saxophonist, but most of his work took place in recording studios, accompanying other musicians as they made their CDs. Tara preferred performing live. She wanted to be out there playing her bass onstage and hearing the cheers of her devoted fans, who would travel enthusiastically across continents to see her, not leave her in the lurch like her parents so often did.

Now, with rock music pounding in her ears, Tara finished stuffing the few remaining possessions into her bag. She lugged it down to reception, where Jimmy was waiting for her, his handsome face beaming. Tara gave him the luggage, and thrust her earphones and player into her pocket.

"All ready?" asked Jimmy.

Tara nodded. Connie and Tambo each gave her a big hug, and told her to take care. Tara had the impression that they didn't really approve of the way her parents had abandoned her either.

"You enjoy your new semester, now," Connie said. "And as soon as you're famous, be sure to send me your first CD."

Jimmy and Tara walked out to the safari lodge's single-engine airplane and clambered in. The small plane was soon bumping and rattling its way over the red earth of the landing strip, and then it was up and gaining height. Once they reached the city airport, Jimmy was going to hand Tara over to the airline escort, who would take care of her on the long international flight.

At the bustling terminal, Jimmy helped Tara check in

her bag. He made sure she had her passport, boarding pass, and carry-on luggage before seeing her through the boarding gate where her escort was waiting. He gave Tara a cheerful smile and a wave, before striding off on more lodge business.

Tara watched him go. She knew her father would have paid Jimmy well for looking after her, but he had been very kind, and she would miss his bad jokes and fantastic animal stories.

By the time Tara landed at Heathrow Airport, Jimmy and Africa seemed a lifetime away. The airline escort had irritated her intensely by treating her like a child, and the constant thrumming of the plane's engines had prevented her from getting any sleep. What with that and her early start, Tara was exhausted. Thank goodness her dad had been as good as his word and had arranged for someone to meet her.

As Tara emerged from customs, she scanned the mass of expectant faces. She spotted a young woman at the barrier who was holding a hurriedly written sign with Tara's name on it.

"Did you have a good flight?" the woman inquired. She didn't wait for an answer, but led the way out to where the car was parked. The woman loaded Tara's bags into the trunk and then started the car. Tara slumped down in the back, and tried to feel happy about returning to school on her own. She should be used to it by now.

Once on the highway, the woman wanted to chat.

"Rockley Park. That's where you go if you want to be a pop singer, isn't it?" she said.

"Or a rock musician," growled Tara, who wasn't a great lover of pop music.

"It must be fun playing music all day," the woman said.

"We don't play music all day," Tara roused herself to explain. "We have all the usual school classes as well. It's actually harder than a normal school."

"Oh." After a moment the woman said, "Do you get to meet lots of famous people?"

But there was no answer. Tara had finally fallen asleep, and she stayed asleep until the car pulled up outside Rockley Park School for the Performing Arts.

"Uh…" she groaned as she crawled out of the car and took her luggage. "I feel terrible. I'm not ready to face anyone at school yet!"

2. Mixed Feelings

Tara struggled along the hallway and into her room, where she dumped her bags by her bed. She was early. The famous model twins, Pop and Lolly Lowther, weren't here yet. Nor was Chloe, her other roommate. But even though it was empty, the room didn't look unlived in. Students at Rockley Park were allowed to leave their possessions at school over spring break, so the beds were made up with their own duvet covers, their books were on the shelves, and favorite posters were on the bulletin boards above their beds.

"Hello, Tara. You're very early." Mrs. Pinto, Tara's housemother, popped her head around the door and smiled at her. "Goodness! Don't you look healthy?

Look at all those adorable freckles. Have you been somewhere nice over spring break?

"Not really," said Tara, not wanting to be questioned about her vacation. "Is anyone else here yet?"

"You're the first," Mrs. Pinto said. "I don't think anyone else will turn up for a while. But you've got some mail. It's in your mailbox downstairs."

Tara nodded.

After Mrs. Pinto had gone, Tara decided she couldn't bear to unpack just yet. She hung up her thin jacket and pulled a sweater out of one of her drawers. She was chilly after her hot week in Africa.

I wonder who's written to me? she thought.

She wandered back along the quiet hallway and went downstairs. In her mailbox was a postcard from her father. Trust him to do that. He could have called or texted her, but he always sent her postcards.

He was still working on the new jazz album and sounded very busy.

"Have a good semester, sweetie," he'd written. "Hope you like our present. Judge Jim Henson will have it for you. Must go. The boys want to fit in another track if they can. Looks like it's going to be another long night."

"Huh!" Tara wasn't very impressed. "That's typical. They always send presents when they've let me down. But why did they send this one to Judge Jim?"

Judge Jim Henson was Head of the Rock Department. He and Tara's father had known each other for years, but that was no reason for her present to be sent to him. What were her parents up to?

Tara stuffed the postcard in her pocket and went over to the Rock Department. Like many of the teachers, Judge Jim got to school early at the beginning of the semester to arrange everything before the students arrived. He was in the main room, changing a plug. A mellow blues-guitar CD was playing on the sound system.

"Hi, Tara!" he greeted her, shaking his gray dreadlocks back from his dark, wrinkled face. "You been sunbathing?"

She ignored his question. "Did something come for me?" she asked, pulling the postcard from her pocket.

Judge Jim was smiling at her. "Sure did. It arrived a couple of hours ago."

Tara frowned. "What is it, then?" she asked. The lavish boxes of chocolates and designer bags and scarves that her mother usually sent hardly needed Judge Jim's attention.

Judge Jim looked surprised. "You don't know?" He put the plug and screwdriver down and got up. "It's in my office. Come and see."

Tara followed as he led the way to his small, cluttered room. There didn't seem to be anything gift-wrapped among the heaps of paperwork on Judge Jim's desk. But her teacher was picking up a large guitar case and putting it carefully on top of the papers.

"Is it your birthday?" he asked, waving her toward the case.

"No," she told him, her hands hesitating over the latches.

"Well, lucky you," he said. "Go on. Open it up!"

Tara undid the case and lifted the lid. Inside, a layer

of wrapping protected the instrument. She pulled it off and saw a beautiful, long-necked, black-and-white bass guitar.

"Oh!"

"It *is* lovely, isn't it?" said Judge Jim.

"A Rickenbacker! I've wanted one forever," Tara enthused.

"Well, now you've got one. Oh, and I advised your dad to get you this." He opened a drawer, took out a lead, and handed it to Tara.

"But I already have a lead for my bass," she said. "Couldn't I use that one?"

"You could," Judge Jim said. "But this lead is rather special. It will let the sound through so much better. Don't lose it. The lead was very expensive, but I told your dad that you and the bass were worth it!"

Tara looked away, unable to speak for a moment. Her parents were always letting her down and then trying to make up for it with presents, but they'd never sent her anything like this. Dad must have asked Judge Jim's advice to get exactly the instrument she wanted.

She was sure she'd never told him how much she admired Rickenbacker basses. Her dad wasn't into guitars.

Tara usually despised the presents her parents sent, but she couldn't possibly despise this one. Her emotions were pulled back and forth, and she wasn't sure how she felt. She should call her dad and thank him, but she was still angry with both parents for ruining her vacation and not taking her back to school themselves. However wonderful the Rickenbacker was, it still didn't make up for them deserting her, and she didn't want them to think it did.

To her annoyance, she felt tears pricking the backs of her eyes. But Tara Fitzgerald *never* cried. She preferred to get angry instead. So her parents sent an expensive present because they felt guilty? That was *their* problem.

Judge Jim seemed to sense her emotion. He squeezed her shoulder. "I have some paperwork to do in here," he said quietly. "Why don't you take your new bass into the main room and get acquainted?"

Tara nodded. Thank goodness her teacher didn't want a long conversation. In spite of being upset with her parents, she couldn't wait to try out the Rickenbacker.

Tara took it through into the other room and connected it up to her amp with the new lead. Nearby, her old bass sat on its stand, looking rather forlorn. She'd missed it so much while she was on safari, but now that she had her new bass she wasn't going to be playing the old one anytime soon. She sniffed defiantly, sat down, and rested the heavy Rickenbacker on her knee. The inlay on the neck was beautiful and the white trim on the black body of the bass looked really elegant. She would have to get a new strap. Her old one was too beat-up.

She wrapped her left hand around the neck and plucked the open strings with the fingers of her right hand. It was almost perfectly in tune. Judge Jim must have tuned it up for her. She corrected the one string that had stretched and gone slightly flat, then she played a minor scale. The deep, rich sound filled the room, but minor scales were too sad. She needed to keep away from the blues. A bit of funk should do it. Yeah. That was better. Forget her parents! They didn't need to think she'd be grateful. But she was very, very pleased with this bass.

Much later, Tara left the Rock Department and made her way back to her dorm. Paddock House was full of noise now, with girls excitedly greeting one another and exchanging news. Pop, Lolly, and Chloe were all in the bedroom, which was a chaotic mess of half-unpacked bags and open closets. Pop and Lolly were models, and never traveled light. It looked as if they'd both brought tons more clothes to school this semester, even though their dressers were already bursting.

"Tara!" yelled Pop, waving her arms dramatically as she always did. "Where have you been? Why haven't you unpacked yet? Have you been to dinner?"

"No," muttered Tara. Pop's wild enthusiasm always made her clam up.

"Did you have a good vacation?" Chloe asked.

Tara shrugged. "It was okay," she said. She lifted her bag onto her bed and began to unpack.

Pop turned to Chloe. "We went to Africa, too!" she told her excitedly, closing her trunk with a slam. "It was all at the last minute, but Tikki Deacon, the supermodel, wanted some younger models on a special shoot she was doing, and she asked for *us*!"

Tara pricked up her ears. Wasn't it Tikki Deacon whom her mom had gone to interview?

"You wouldn't believe the security she had," said Lolly. "I think it was totally over-the-top, but she's such a big name I guess she thinks she needs lots of bodyguards. We saw your mom, too," Lolly added to Tara. "What a coincidence! I asked if you were around, but she said you were with your dad." Lolly shook her head. "Your poor mom!" she told Tara. "She does work hard. She was trying her best to get an interview with Tikki, but she didn't have a hope during the shoot. Afterward we all went to the beach for a couple of days, and Tikki invited her to join us, so she got her interview in the end."

Tara tried to concentrate on her unpacking, rather than listening to the twins, but it was impossible. Now she was really angry. Why hadn't her mom let her know that the twins were there? That was so typical of her mom. She must have realized Pop and Lolly would bring it up.

"You should have brought your dad and come also," Pop told Tara. "The beach was great!" She grinned.

Tara sniffed, and busied herself putting her clothes away. Pop glanced at her sister, frowning at Tara's lack of response.

Lolly tried again. "We heard you were on safari," she said. "That must have been fun, too."

"Safari!" squeaked Chloe. "How fantastic. The farthest away I've ever been is a cabin in the countryside! Just think," she added rather sadly, "I'm the only one in our room who's never been out of this country."

Tara yanked some grubby shirts out of her bag and hurled them onto the floor to take along to the laundry room.

"You don't know what it was like," she snapped bitterly. "And," she continued, rounding on Pop and

27

Lolly, "while you were having fun together, I was on my own with a bunch of boring adults. If I'd known, I'd have loved to have come to the coast. But Mom was obviously enjoying herself way too much to want *me* with her."

The shocked expressions on her friends' faces aggravated Tara even more.

"I had to come all the way back to England by myself," she told them angrily. "You don't know how lucky you are with your families. I might as well be an orphan!"

The truth of what she had said hit Tara, and she bit her lip. But she wouldn't cry, not now or ever. Crying wasn't what Tara Fitzgerald did.

3. A Good Idea?

"Why did you have to go all the way to Africa for a fashion shoot?" Chloe asked the twins, hurriedly changing the subject.

"Oh, magazines like exotic locations," Pop told her. "Luckily for us! We'd never been to Africa before."

"Apparently, Tikki only did this shoot because she was allowed to choose the location," Lolly added.

"Typical!" snorted Tara.

"Well, that's what I would've thought," Lolly said. "Tikki Deacon *can* act as if she's the only one in the world who's important, but it wasn't like that at all. We didn't realize, but she's involved in a charity that helps orphaned children in Africa, and she wanted to visit to see the work they do."

"We did the shoot at their school," said Pop. "It's a boarding school, but nothing like Rockley Park. For a start, because the children are orphaned, they live there all the time. It's their home as well as a school. But they were amazing kids. They've all had a horrible time, but they were so friendly and welcoming when we arrived."

"I felt really guilty modeling all those expensive clothes, while most of the children didn't even have any shoes," said Lolly.

"But Tikki said that was the point," Pop reminded her twin. "She hoped the contrast would really make people think. And she'd been promised a write-up and loads of publicity about the school to go with the pictures."

"She thinks if being famous can sell clothes, it should be able to get attention for more important things, too," added Lolly. "Like raising money for the orphans' school. I hope she's right. Those children need all the help they can get."

"There was one little boy named Nangila who really latched on to Lolly," said Pop. "His dad had been killed in the war, and he lost his mom and baby sister, too, before the charity found him all alone."

"That's terrible," Chloe said quietly. "I can't imagine what it would feel like to lose my whole family."

"I know," Lolly agreed. "And the awful thing is, Tikki said that there are lots more children who need help, but the charity doesn't have enough space or money to look after any more at the moment. They're struggling even to keep the place open. I've got some pictures we took," she went on, rummaging in her bag. "Here they are. Look."

Pop and Lolly's trip sounded much more worthwhile than the time Tara had spent with a bunch of wealthy tourists. She wanted to see the pictures too. "Let's see," she said. She abandoned all pretense of unpacking and joined the others.

Lolly passed the photographs around. There was one of Tikki Deacon surrounded by her entourage of bodyguards and another of a cameraman grinning as he had his picture taken. Then there were loads of photos of the children.

"It looks so hot and dusty," said Chloe as Lolly held out a picture of a shyly smiling little boy holding her hand. "Oh! Isn't he sweet?" The child had bare, dusty feet and was wearing a pair of shorts that looked too big for his skinny body. His T-shirt was faded and torn.

"That's Nangila," said Lolly.

Tara stared at the picture. The child was standing in front of a simple building with a tin roof. He obviously needed clothes and shoes, for a start. He was smiling, but when Tara looked at his eyes she could see that they were full of loneliness. Yes, he'd been rescued, but he still didn't have most of the things she took for granted. And Tara got lonely with her parents away so much, but that was *nothing* compared to Nangila's pain. A wave of anger washed through her.

"We should do something for those kids," she muttered.

"That's a good idea!" said Pop enthusiastically.

"What do you think we should do?" Chloe asked.

"Raise money, or send them stuff...?" Before Tara could reply, Lolly was speaking.

"I promised I'd send them copies of these pictures once I'd printed them all out," she said. "They were so excited to have their pictures taken." Then she shrugged. "It doesn't seem like much, but I thought it might help a little for them to know we hadn't forgotten them."

Tara sniffed. "You're right," she said witheringly. "A few pictures *aren't* very much. I could do a *lot* better than that! They need real help!"

Lolly blushed and Chloe frowned at Tara.

"Yes, you're right," said Lolly quietly. "We've got so much, and they have hardly anything. We should raise some money for them or do *something* to help. What do you think we should do, Tara?"

Everyone looked at Tara.

Tara hesitated. She didn't have a clue about orphaned children, and she had no experience raising money for charity. She needed time to think.

"Well?" demanded Pop, who hated to be kept waiting, even for a few seconds.

"Let's go and have dinner," said Tara suddenly. "It must be time."

"But what do you think we should do?" asked Chloe.

"I'll tell you over dinner," Tara told her grandly. She snatched the photograph of Nangila out of Lolly's hand and made for the door. She simply *had* to come up with a good plan.

She didn't wait for the others, but shot down the stairs, clutching the picture. She glanced at it as she raced over to the dining room. The face of the child was haunting her. What if it was *her* in the picture with torn clothes and bare feet? How could she bear it? What if *her* parents were killed in an accident or something? Her wish to see them was like a sudden physical pain, but she tried to bury her feelings. Of course they were fine. All the same, she would text them right after dinner, just to make sure.

She glanced at the picture of little Nangila again. She shouldn't feel sorry for herself. She really shouldn't. She should be thinking of *him.*

4. Tara's Idea

Once in the dining room, Tara made for their usual table, thinking hard. If only she could come up with a clever fund-raising idea, she might be able to help that orphaned boy and others like him.

A minute later the others arrived, and Pop zoomed over to the buffet.

"It's your favorite!" Pop yelled to her sister. But Lolly and Chloe had seen Danny James with some more of their friends and were waving them over.

"Come and sit down," Chloe invited the boys. "Tara, move into the middle so you can explain your idea. Did you bring the rest of the pictures, Lolly?"

"What's all this about?" asked Ed Henderson. He

and Ben Peters, who were both guitarists, sat down.

"Tara's had this amazing idea," announced Pop, plonking her tray down and slopping juice everywhere. "But we don't know much about it yet."

"Well, wait until we've got our dinner," said Danny, who was a drummer. He and Marmalade Stamp, the only dancer in the group of friends, went to get some food. For a few minutes everyone was busy figuring out what they wanted to eat and drink, and catching up on spring-break gossip. But as soon as they were all settled, Pop waved at Tara, dangerously close to spilling her drink again.

"Come on, Tara," she urged. "Tell us about your idea."

"Show them the pictures," said Tara, still stalling. So Lolly mopped up Pop's earlier spills, then spread the photos out on the table.

"We were doing a fashion shoot in Africa over the break," Lolly explained. "The children in these pictures are all orphans, and Tara thinks we could do something to help them."

"It just doesn't seem fair that we have so much and they have nothing," explained Tara, feeling angry all over again as she looked at the pictures.

"Fair enough," agreed Marmalade, looking at Tara curiously. "So what's your idea?"

"Well..." Tara said, still thinking furiously. "Some of us have tons of clothes." She glanced at the twins. "We could send clothes, or toys, books... I wasn't there, but you can see from the pictures that they don't have much, and they are orphans." She paused and then began again firmly. "My parents gave me a new bass this term. I'm going to start by selling my old one to raise money for the children."

"Wow!" said Ed. "That's generous, Tara. I've got three guitars, but I don't think I could bear to part with *any* of them!"

Tara shrugged. "You can only play one at a time," she said. "But that's just me," she hurried on, seeing his face fall. "I'm sure we can all find *something* to sell that we don't want anymore."

"Maybe we could make things, too," said Chloe.

"Do you think Mrs. Pinto would let us use the kitchen in our dorm to make cakes to sell?"

"I'm no good at cooking," admitted Marmalade. "But I could do a sponsored pirouette!"

"You need sponsoring *not* to do that," Tara told him crushingly. "You're always spinning around on one leg, getting in the way."

"But a sponsored event *could* work," objected Lolly.

"I suppose," Tara hastily agreed, realizing that putting Marmalade down wasn't going to win her any support. "Thanks."

Marmalade, who was pretty irrepressible, raised his eyebrows at Tara's mood change. "Miss Fitzgerald is being nice," he observed. "How cool is that? Does she want something?"

Tara scowled at him. "I want sensible suggestions," she told him angrily.

"I thought all this was supposed to be *your* brilliant idea," he said.

"I know!" said Pop, ignoring the last remark to Tara's

great relief. "Marmalade could get sponsored to stay sensible for as long as possible!"

Everyone laughed except for Marmalade and Tara.

"It was a *joke*!" Pop told him. "You're not the only one who can crack them."

"But this is serious," Tara said, looking at the pictures on the table. "And actually I don't think that a sale, or sponsoring each other, will raise enough money. Even selling my bass probably won't make very much. I think we need something else to get money in from outside the school. *Lots* of it," she added firmly. "Wouldn't it be great if we could send tons of money?" She held up the picture of the little boy with the sad eyes. "Maybe the charity would be able to rescue more children like Nangila, then."

Everyone was quiet for a few moments. Then an idea flipped into Tara's head. It was so good and so simple that it made her catch her breath. "I know!" she said. "I've got the perfect idea."

"Oh yeah?" mocked Marmalade. "Another one?"

"What?" asked Chloe.

"Well, what are we all good at?" Tara demanded, excitement rising in her by the second.

Chloe shrugged. "I don't know," she mused. "I'm good at English..."

"And I like biology, but what use is that?" added Lolly.

"No! I don't mean schoolwork. What are we *here* for?" Tara demanded.

Pop squealed excitedly. "I know. Music, of course!"

"Exactly," Tara agreed. "Music. Why not sell what we do best?"

Now she really had their attention. "We could play some songs," she told them, her mind racing. "Get Mr. Timms to record them and make a CD. Then we get lots of them copied, ask the art department to design the covers, and we sell them ...everywhere." She sat back, pleased and relieved that she'd come up with such a good idea.

"Who's going to buy them, though?" asked Ed. "I mean, really? We might sell a few to friends and parents, but it won't raise that much money."

Tara looked at him impatiently. "So we get some famous names to join us," she told him. "Mr. Player was a pop singer before he came here to give voice lessons. I bet tons of people our parents' age will remember him. And what about Judge Jim?"

Everyone nodded. To ask the Head of the Rock Department was a seriously good idea. He was famous all over the world.

"Where would we sell the CDs?" asked Ben. "Do you think we could get them into music stores?"

"Of course!" Tara told him airily. "All it needs is a little organization."

"Who's going to do all that?" asked Chloe.

"All what?" demanded Tara.

"The organization," Lolly put in. "It'll take a lot of work. Of course, I'll help. I think we all will. But someone will have to be in charge."

"Well, that'll be Tara, obviously," said Pop. "It was her idea, after all. When are you going to get started?" she added, looking at Tara.

"Yeah," Ben said. "You'll have to let us know how

many songs you want, who's going to do them, and things like that."

"And you'll have to ask Mr. Timms's permission to use the recording studio," added Ed.

"I know!" Tara told him angrily.

She was beginning to wish she hadn't come up with the idea, if everyone was going to nag her about it. And there was never much time to spare at Rockley Park School. By the time classes and homework were done, and preparation for the regular school concerts fit in, it would be hard to find time to organize a charity CD as well.

"So when are you going to go and see him?" Ed insisted.

Tara was just about to snap. She almost told Ed to do it himself if he was so eager. Then she glanced at the picture of Nangila again and her determination came flooding back.

"Tomorrow," she told Ed firmly. "I'll go and see Mr. Timms right after breakfast."

5. A Difficult Task

When Tara went to the studio the next morning, Mr. Timms was in the tiny kitchen next door.

"I need to make a CD," Tara announced without any preamble. Mr. Timms glanced at her and motioned for her to get out of the way.

"Not enough...room," he muttered testily. Tara retreated to the doorway and waited while he made his coffee and searched for some fresh milk in the fridge. "Now," he said at last, shooing her in front of him. "Go...on..."

He followed her through to the control room.

Tara hadn't had much occasion to be in here, and she looked around with interest at the large mixing desk with its rows of knobs and faders, and the computer screens off to one side. The room was packed full of equipment, and there was only space for a couple of chairs at the desk. Through the glass partitions were the two soundproofed booths where the singers and musicians performed and were recorded. Although Tara preferred playing rather than studying the finer points of engineering good music, studios were a vital part of the music industry, and this one was an exciting place to be. Mr. Timms was admired by everyone as an excellent recording engineer, even though he looked like someone who'd rather be at home in his slippers than pushing back the frontiers of modern music technology.

He sat in a chair with a gray cardigan hanging over it and put his mug down carefully.

"What do you need to record?" he asked.

"Songs for a charity CD," she told him importantly. "It's for children in Africa and we're all going to do something and record lots of songs and get Judge Jim and Mr. Player involved as well and sell it to tons of people and it's really important." She paused for a breath, and waited for him to tell her when they could record, but instead he took a long sip of coffee and stared into space.

"I think I'll play with Danny, Ed, and Ben," Tara added. "We haven't decided what to record yet, but I thought I should come and tell you first so that you can—"

"So it's not really a school project?" Mr. Timms interrupted.

"Well, no," she admitted. "But it'll be—"

"Can't do it," he muttered.

Tara stared at him. "But—"

"Can't do it," he repeated, swiveling in his chair and flicking a few switches on the mixing desk. "Any nonschool projects have to be approved by the, er... principal. You'll have to see Mrs. Sharkey before ..."

The teacher's mutterings were getting on Tara's nerves. And what was worse, he was ignoring her now, expecting her to go. But Tara wasn't prepared to leave it at that. She stood up and folded her arms.

"So you'll help when Mrs. Sharkey has agreed, right?" she demanded.

Mr. Timms swiveled his chair back toward Tara. "Every now and then someone has an idea like yours," he told her. "They get all excited about it for five minutes and then, when they realize how much hard work it will be, they lose interest." He looked at her pointedly. "Are you ... in charge?" he asked.

Tara nodded firmly.

"You'll need plenty of ... push," he told her.

"So you *will* help?"

"Don't waste studio time," he told her. Tara was going to protest, but Mr. Timms hadn't finished. "Get them here on time ... don't let them mess around ... keep control. It's the only way ..."

But Tara wasn't listening anymore. "Thanks!" she said, already heading for the door. "I'll be back!"

Tara had to wait until classes finished at lunchtime before she could go and see Mrs. Sharkey.

"I'm sorry, dear," the principal's secretary told her.

"Mrs. Sharkey is away today. I'll make an appointment for you to see her tomorrow."

Tara had to swallow her disappointment, but she didn't intend to let her idea drop. That evening, after homework had been done, Chloe found her at the dorm computer.

"What are you doing?" Chloe asked.

"I looked up Tikki Deacon's charity on the Internet," Tara told her. "And it's all here. The school where they did the fashion shoot can only take care of fifty children, and according to this there are *thousands* who need the same help, but there just isn't the money to do it. And that school *does* need more money urgently or it might have to close."

"That's terrible," said Chloe. "It won't close now, though, with Tikki Deacon helping, will it?"

"I don't know," Tara told her. "In my experience, adults often let you down. Who knows? She might support them for a few weeks and then go on to something else. But the school needs help all the time." She thought for a moment and then turned to face Chloe. "When I see Mrs. Sharkey tomorrow, I'm going to ask if we can adopt the charity, and make it our job to help keep the school going."

"What an awesome idea!" said Chloe.

By the time her meeting with Mrs. Sharkey arrived, Tara had gotten one of the office staff to make a large photocopy of the picture that had so touched her heart, and had printed out a lot of information about the charity that was running the African school. Since seeing Mr. Timms, she had organized her thoughts much better, but even so, she was quite nervous as the secretary showed her into the principal's office.

Mrs. Sharkey was sitting behind an enormous, polished wooden desk, wearing one of her alarming tweed suits.

Tara took the blown-up photograph and information from under her arm, and placed it on the desk, facing the principal.

"We want to produce a charity CD for this little boy

and others like him," Tara explained, trying to keep her voice firm. "His school might close if they don't get more help, and none of the children has parents. They *live* there. That school is their *home.*"

"Very laudable," Mrs. Sharkey acknowledged. "How do you know about the school?"

Tara explained about Pop and Lolly's fashion shoot, and then she showed Mrs. Sharkey everything she'd printed out from the charity's Web site. "They're struggling to stay open," said Tara, fired with indignation. "What will happen to Nangila if the school has to close?"

"I can see how passionate you are about this," Mrs. Sharkey said. "Is it all up to you, or are others prepared to be involved?"

"Lots of people want to help," said Tara. "But I'm in charge."

"I see." Mrs. Sharkey looked at Tara. "Do you realize how much work it would be, producing a CD?" she asked. But before Tara could answer, Mrs. Sharkey spoke again. "It's not just all the time it would take to actually record the songs," she said. "A good deal of administration is involved in a project like this. Even just taking orders from students and their families and collecting the money is very time-consuming."

Tara rushed to reply. "I don't mind. It's *important.*"

Mrs. Sharkey nodded. "Yes, you're right," she agreed. "Every child *is* important, whoever they are, and wherever they live. I'm pleased to see you care so passionately for the welfare of others. But my job is to worry about *your* welfare, and I wonder if producing a CD might be a bit *too* ambitious. Remember, we have a school concert scheduled for midterm. Students will want to concentrate on that because everyone will be evaluated at it. Then there's the televised Rising Stars concert at the end of the semester for the lucky few who are the best performers. You've chosen the busiest term of the whole year."

"I know," said Tara. "But Judge Jim has told me not to try out for the Rising Stars concert this time. He wants me to concentrate on my technique for a while longer." She looked earnestly at the principal. "That means I can easily do most of the work for the CD!"

Mrs. Sharkey shook her head. "It would still be a lot for one person to take on," she told her. "And there are all the other students to consider, too. Why not have a collection at school instead? If the charity is a good one, I would even give you permission to ask the parents to contribute when they come to the midterm concert. That way it wouldn't take too much time away from your studies, and yet would still be helping what looks like a very worthy cause."

Tara stared at the principal. "But that won't raise enough!" she objected. "A CD could raise thousands!"

Mrs. Sharkey smiled regretfully at her. "I'm afraid you have a rather inflated idea of how much money a CD might raise," she said. "You may all be very talented students, but you're not mainstream artists yet. The most you could hope for would be sales to friends and relatives. The money raised might not be very much at all after you'd paid for the CDs to be copied. In fact, it might not even be as much as you'd raise by taking a collection."

"I'd still like to try," said Tara stubbornly.

"I know," Mrs. Sharkey replied, seeing the expression on Tara's face, "you think I'm being deliberately obstructive, but I've had students coming to me with similar ideas before, and every one of them failed."

Tara set her mouth stubbornly. "But *I* won't fail," she told the principal.

Mrs. Sharkey smiled. "That's the attitude you need to succeed," she said. "But I can't just let you go ahead and hope for the best. I'll tell you what I'll do," she went on as Tara started to object again. "Leave me the information about the charity and I'll have a good look at it. In fact, I had been thinking we should partner this school with another, in a disadvantaged area—"

"I was going to ask about adopting the school!" Tara butted in.

Mrs. Sharkey held up her hand for silence. "In addition," she said, "if you can come back to me with a properly planned list of, let's say, a minimum of twelve potential tracks, and the names of students who have agreed to perform them for the CD, I'll think seriously about giving you permission to do it. But I'm telling you now that it will be a lot of work, and when you think it through you may consider that you simply can't devote enough time to it. I admire you for thinking of it, though," she added, and handed Tara back the photograph.

Tara took the picture and left in a determined mood.

Mrs. Sharkey can't be right, she thought on her way back downstairs. *I* must *be able to raise more money with a CD than a simple collection. And I can* easily *find twelve songs and people to sing them. In fact, I'll start right now!*

6. A Difficult Time

Tara strode into the dining room. She'd been with Mrs. Sharkey for quite a while, so by the time she'd chosen her lunch and sat down at the usual table, only Danny and Marmalade were still there.

"Where is everyone?" she asked, disappointed not to see the table full so she could talk to everyone at once.

"I think the girls have gone back to your dorm," Danny told her. "Ed and Ben are outside, talking guitars as usual."

"Oh. Well, I'll talk to them later," said Tara, picking at her salad. "You can both give me your commitment first."

"What commitment?" asked Marmalade suspiciously. "I'm not sure I like the sound of that."

"It's all right," Tara reassured him. "I'm just looking for some tracks and artists for my charity CD, and I need you to agree to do one."

"I'm a dancer, Tara," Marmalade reminded her.

"I *know* that," she replied. "But you sing as well. Get some friends to help if you don't want to sing on your own. Sign here." She opened a notebook and offered him her pen.

"I'll sign, Tara," Danny offered. "You know me. I'm always up to perform something. Just let me know what, and I'll drum for you."

"Thanks!" Tara watched as he signed his name. "Once I've got enough people, we can discuss exactly what we're going to do."

"Oh, all right," said Marmalade, taking the pen from Danny. "I'll help. It is a good cause."

"Great." Tara was pleased. She'd only been trying for five minutes and she'd signed the first two people she'd asked. This was going to be easy. She'd soon have the tracks chosen, and then Mrs. Sharkey would *have* to give her the go-ahead.

But as the afternoon went on, it became obvious that it wasn't going to be quite that simple. Although Ben and Ed were happy to help out, too, there was bad news when Tara got back to her room at the end of the day.

"We've just had a singing lesson and Mr. Player has told us we're not allowed to do *anything* that might distract us from winning Rising Stars points," said Pop. "If we're going to have a chance at performing in the Rising Stars concert, we need all the points we can get, and the midterm concert is *vital* for that."

"This is terrible," said Lolly, looking very distressed. "I really wanted to contribute. There must be something we can do."

"Only if Mr. Player doesn't hear about it," warned Pop. "He said we should be practicing twenty-four hours a day!"

"Even Mr. Player can't expect *that*!" said Tara.

"Maybe I should wait until I have my lesson with Mr.

Player, too, before I volunteer to sing for you," said Chloe, looking worried.

Tara slumped down on her bed and frowned. She could see that Rising Stars points, and the concerts, were going to be a real problem.

Throughout the year, students were awarded Rising Stars points for their progress in music classes and concert performances, and the upcoming midterm concert was the last chance for students to earn more points. Afterward, a final decision would be made about who would appear in the all-important Rising Stars concert. This was always recorded at the local TV station in front of an invited audience of important people from the music business, and it only happened once a year. Not only was it really exciting to have the concert shown on local television, some students had been signed to record companies after Rising Stars concerts. Only the top students would be chosen to perform, but everyone was desperate to take part.

"Can't we do a charity CD *next* semester?" suggested Pop. "I really want to be involved. After all, if we hadn't told you about it, you'd never have known about Nangila's school."

"But it needs help *now*," objected Tara. "It says on the Web site that the school might close if they don't get more funding. The children can't hang around until after you get your precious points."

"That's true," agreed Lolly sadly. "But Mr. Player will be *furious* if he finds out that we've ignored what he said."

Tara stomped out of the room and went downstairs, too angry and upset to stay with the others. She wanted to blame her friends for not agreeing right away to help with the CD, but deep inside she could understand. Even if it was making her efforts to raise money for Nangila's school harder.

On an impulse she pulled her phone out of her pocket and began to write a text. Her mom knew all about raising money for charity, as she often reported on glittering charity fund-raisers for her magazine. Maybe she would have some idea how Tara could get the CD plan to work. *How do you get lots of people to support a charity idea?* she texted. *Help! I need to know urgently for something I want to do.* Then she pressed send and hoped for a useful reply.

Tara had started to calm down, so she went back to her room. She took the blown-up picture of Nangila and Lolly, and stuck it up over her bed, as a reminder that she shouldn't give up.

It was much too late to go over to the Rock Department, but Tara was fidgety. She wanted to *do* something for her cause *now*. She picked up a notebook and pencil and threw herself onto the end of her bed. She would try writing a song for Nangila. She liked writing songs. All her anger and desire to help the orphaned children could be poured out onto the page. Maybe, if it was good enough, it would be one for the CD.

Tara turned over and lay on her back, staring up at the picture on the wall. It was Nangila's eyes that got her every time.

Eyes...skies... She doodled with her pencil, resting the notebook on her raised knees. *Lies...flies.* What else? *Pain...gain...chain.* She rolled over onto her front again and concentrated hard.

Pain in his eyes, she wrote. No, that wasn't quite right. *Pain in your eyes.* Better. She scribbled furiously, crossing out as she went. In a few minutes, she had the beginnings of some lyrics she liked. She wrote them out again and then read them over to herself.

Don't tell me no lies.

I see the pain in your eyes.

Yes. That was right. And in her head she could hear a deep, chugging, funky intro to the song on her bass. The fingers of her left hand twitched and she could almost feel them on the glossy neck of her beautiful new guitar.

I see the pain in your eyes, she whispered to Nangila reassuringly. *And however difficult it is, I'm going to help keep you safe at your school. I promise.*

7. Tara's Song

At Rockley Park, the students had classes on Saturday mornings and gym in the afternoon. But Sundays were all about relaxing.

"What are you doing, Tara?" asked Chloe as they all lounged around in their room after Sunday lunch. "It's not homework, is it?"

Tara looked up from her notebook and smiled. She was feeling quite happy today. "It's a song I'm writing," she explained. "I'm going over to the Rock Department later to try it out."

"What's it about?" asked Chloe. "You seem to have been working very hard on it."

Tara nodded. "Yes, but I think it's going to be worth

it. It's about him." She pointed up to the picture on the wall above her bed. "If the song is good enough, I'll put it on the charity CD. I'm still going to ask Judge Jim if he'll cut a track for the CD as well," Tara added. "If I'm lucky, I might even see him this afternoon."

There was usually a movie to watch on Sunday evening, and it was always very popular. But Tara wasn't interested today. After gulping down a quick dinner, she headed over to the Rock Department. Everyone else would be going to watch the movie, so she should have the place to herself.

As she opened the door to the building, she could hear that there were still a couple of people in the main room. She groaned with annoyance. There was no mistaking Ed's trademark guitar wail. He and Ben were jamming. Had they forgotten about dinner?

Tara *could* have taken her Rickenbacker into one of the small side rooms, but she didn't like playing cooped up in a tight space, and she didn't like not getting her own way either.

"Time for dinner!" she yelled at the two boys, who

were rocking away together. Ben nodded, and continued playing. Ed hadn't even noticed her.

Tara strode over to the boys' amps and unplugged both their guitars. Silence reigned. But not for long.

"Hey!"

"What'd you do *that* for?"

Ed put his guitar down on its stand and reached for the lead. Tara spun away from him, still holding it.

"Careful," warned Ben. "It's still plugged into his guitar." He quickly unplugged his own guitar and set it down. "What's up, Tara?"

Tara handed Ed his lead.

"It's dinnertime," she said again. "If you don't hurry, you'll miss it."

Ben pointed to some empty potato-chip bags and soda cans on a nearby chair.

"We don't want dinner," he told her. "We went to the snack shop yesterday and stocked up."

"But the movie will start soon," she objected.

"Why are you so concerned about us all of a sudden?" demanded Ed. "We don't want to watch the movie this week. It's a really girlie one. We're not interested."

"Yeah," agreed Ben. "We were enjoying ourselves here. If you want to play, why not join in? It would help to have you on your cool new bass anyway. You didn't have to unplug us."

"I don't want to jam," Tara told them. "I want to work something out."

"Well, go and use a practice room. That's what they're for," Ed told her.

Tara felt like stamping her foot. But that wouldn't get her anywhere. The boys were completely within their rights to be here.

She was just trying to come up with a convincing reason why they should give way to her unreasonable demands when the door banged. Tara's heart sank. Now someone *else* was coming! Didn't *anyone* want to watch the movie?

It was Danny, clutching his drumsticks. "I haven't missed anything, have I?" he said to Tara. "Chloe said you'd been working on your song all day and

64

Marmalade told me you'd all come over here. How's it going?" He paused, seeing their bemused faces.

"How's what going?" asked Ben.

"The song for the charity CD," Danny said, starting to look a little confused himself. "Isn't that why you're all over here? I did tell you I'd help with the CD, Tara."

"Yes, you did," replied Tara. "But I didn't ask any of you to come over *today*." She looked at Danny awkwardly. "I was just going to try something I've written. It might not be any good."

"Oh. Sorry." Danny looked embarrassed.

"You didn't tell *me* about your song," said Ed accusingly.

"Or me," added Ben. "Let's see what you have."

"Well ..." Tara pulled her notebook out of her pocket. "I've got a couple of verses, and an idea for a bass intro."

She pushed the chip bags onto the floor and smoothed the notebook onto the chair.

"'Lonely eyes,'" Danny read over her shoulder. "Nice. Are you going to use that as the hook, as well as the title?"

"I think so," Tara agreed. "But it sounds like a ballad, and I don't want that. I want it mostly to be tough, like those kids have to be. It's got to rock."

Ben plugged his guitar back in and played a haunting riff of high notes, then stopped.

"I worked that out during our last songwriting class," he told her. "But I still don't have any words to go with it. If you want, you could use it as a bridge between a couple of the verses, to give a change of mood."

He played it again.

Tara went over to her bass and plugged in. Ben's riff *would* make a great bridge. And if she altered her intro a bit, she could repeat that after he'd played the bridge. Now they just needed a good strong melody for the verses.

"Let's just play," she suggested. "I'll do my intro, and then we'll see where we end up."

Danny came up with a rousing beat right away, and it wasn't long before the two guitarists and Tara on bass were developing it into some classic rock.

"Do we need a chorus?" asked Ed at one point.

"I don't think we do," replied Tara. "We can repeat the hook, 'lonely eyes, pain in your eyes,' at the beginning, at the end of each verse, and after Ben's bridge. That's as much of a chorus as we need, really."

Time flew by, the friends were so involved, and when the door opened again, no one noticed. Judge Jim had come to lock up, but he waited until they had played the song all the way through. When they'd finished, he applauded loudly.

"Well," he said, smiling with approval. "That's one cool song. I love the contrast between the verses and the bridge." He went over to the piano and picked out the tune with his right hand. "Have you thought about harmonizin' your voices for the bridge?"

"No," said Tara.

"Well, you could consider it. Your voice works well with Ed's, Tara." Judge Jim played a few more notes. "Somethin' like that, maybe. It would make it even more poignant after that powerful tune you're usin' for the verses." He looked at his watch and shook his head.

"You have to finish for now, though. Sorry, but I

reckon you should be in your dorms. You don't want to get into trouble for bein' late."

"Wow! Is that the time?" said Ben. "I had no idea."

"We'd better get going," agreed Ed. "Thanks, Tara," he added. "That was great."

"Yeah, thanks, Tara," said Ben, unplugging and putting his guitar away.

"See you in the morning," said Danny as all the boys headed out of the door.

Tara lifted her shoulder strap over her head and laid the Rickenbacker carefully on its rest. The euphoria of the evening was quickly seeping away, and she felt unaccountably sad.

"Do you know anyone who might like to buy my old bass?" she asked Judge Jim, remembering her vow to sell it.

Judge Jim looked surprised. "Don't you want to hang on to it?" he asked. "It's the one you first learned on, isn't it?"

"Yes, but I can only play one bass at a time," she told him.

He looked at her curiously, but didn't object. "I'll see what I can do," he said. "Wait a moment," he added as she made for the door. "My car is parked near Paddock House. I'll walk over with you."

Tara shrugged, but she waited while he turned out the lights and locked the door. The Rock Department had a building all to itself, tucked away to one side of Rockley Park House, so it was quite a walk to get to Tara's dormitory. Judge Jim lived nearby in the next village.

As they walked, Judge Jim chatted about the song, praising the way the friends had been working on it together. They were almost at Paddock House when he paused, and looked at Tara with concern.

"Reckon you were playin' that song right from your heart," he said. He didn't seem to expect an answer, and Tara was feeling too down to reply. "Sometimes you get a lift makin' music," Judge Jim continued. "And sometimes when it's over you're left feelin' empty inside. You were givin' that song everythin' you had," he told her. "And it's a sad song.

The bridge really tugs at your heartstrings, and you sing and play it wonderfully."

Tara nodded in thanks, but couldn't speak. Somehow, Judge Jim had recognized exactly how she felt.

"You're a true artist, Tara," Judge Jim said quietly. "Reckon you'll be well on the way to Risin' Stars status next year if you keep producin' work of this standard. Your father must be really proud."

"He never hears me play!" she burst out in spite of herself. "He doesn't care *what* I do." Her voice broke and she bit her lip.

Judge Jim patted her shoulder. "He's a musician," he said. "I know it's hard, but he has to follow his star, just like you. Use that emotion," he added. "Make it work for you like you have tonight."

Tara nodded, but she was too choked up to reply.

8. Judge Jim's Advice

Tara couldn't afford to stay unhappy if she was going to make good on her promise to help Nangila and his friends, so the next afternoon she decided it was time to summon up her courage and ask Judge Jim to record a track for her CD.

She went over to the Rock Department and knocked on Judge Jim's office door. When he called her in she could see he was in the middle of his ever-present paperwork. He pushed it to one side with obvious relief and smiled at her. That was a good sign.

"Hi there, Tara," he said. "How are you doin'? I don't have a buyer for your bass yet, but I'm seein' someone tomorrow who might take it off your hands."

"Thanks," she said. "But I didn't come to see you about that. I wanted to ask your help. It's about a charity CD I want to do."

"Ah." Judge Jim nodded. "Is that why you want to sell your bass, to raise money for charity?"

"Well, yes," admitted Tara.

"What sort of help do you want?" he asked. "And who's it for? Have you been to ask Mrs. Sharkey?"

"Yes, I have," Tara said. She explained about the children, and their threatened school.

"It's a mighty fine idea if you can pull it together," Judge Jim agreed. "Charity CDs, and concerts, are a great way for the music community to help out."

That was good news! Tara took a deep breath. "I was wondering," she continued, "if you'd like, or be able, or have time to play for the CD..."

Judge Jim waved a hand dismissively. "A concert first is better," he advised her. "Then you can record it live. You'll be able to sell the CD to everyone who performed, everyone who attended, and those who wish they'd gone! That's a lot better than makin' a CD on its own."

"But I can't hold a concert!" protested Tara. "There's already the midterm concert and the Rising Stars one at the end of the semester. There's no time for another one!"

Judge Jim raised his eyebrows. "I'm surprised at you, Tara," he said. "You're not thinkin' straight. I'm sure Mrs. Sharkey would be happy for you to use the midterm concert to raise money for charity. Shake a couple of buckets at parents on the way out and you'll be surprised how much you raise."

Tara sighed. "That's what Mrs. Sharkey said," she admitted.

"There you are, then!" said Judge Jim with a smile.

"But I thought a CD would raise more," said Tara.

"On their own, charity CDs can be a bit hit-or-miss," Judge Jim said. "But if you ask Mr. Timms to record the midterm concert and then sell the CD like I said, as a souvenir, I'm sure you'll do very well with it. I'll buy one!"

"Thanks!" said Tara, a smile creeping over her usually serious face. This conversation hadn't exactly gone the way she'd wanted, but Judge Jim had shown her the way to have the best of both worlds! A money-raising concert *and* a CD. She should be able to raise *tons* for Nangila's school at this rate!

On her way back toward the main house, her phone beeped. It was a message from her mom.

Your project sounds interesting, said the text. *But charity events need lots of publicity to get enough people to attend. Then it should go off without a hitch.*

Tara sat on a low wall and scuffed her sneakers in the gravel on the path while she replied.

So will you and Dad come? she texted. *It's going to be the concert at midterm.* The answer came right back. Her mom must be between meetings.

I'll ask Dad, it said. *But you'd better count us out. The schedule is full just then. Good luck, though, sweetie. We'll be thinking of you. xx*

"Yeah, right!" muttered Tara, kicking a bit of gravel into a nearby flower border. "That's typical! Nothing I do means *anything* to them!"

9. Another Good Idea

But Tara wasn't going to let her mom's reply get her down. She needed to stay focused. She would have to go and see Mr. Timms again to ask if he would record the concert for her, and she had to decide what type of publicity would be best to help the concert raise as much money as possible.

"Hey, Tara!" Tara looked up. It was Danny. "Are you all right?" he asked.

Tara nodded. "Just thinking about what Judge Jim said about fund-raising for Nangila's school."

Danny joined her on the wall. "What did he say?"

"He suggested that we raise money by taking a collection at the midterm concert *and* record the concert for a CD to sell afterward to raise even more money."

Danny rattled his drumsticks along the wall. "Great idea!" he said.

"Yes, it is," agreed Tara. "And if we include as many people as possible, they'll bring their friends along and that would make it into even more of a fund-raiser."

"But we'll all be included anyway, if it's the midterm concert," said Danny.

"I know," said Tara. "But there are the teachers as well. I'm going to ask *them* if they want to join in. It would be so cool if Judge Jim and your drum teacher and a couple of the others would perform together."

"Wow. Yeah!" agreed Danny enthusiastically. "Who else can we think of?" He leaned down and poked the gravel around with the end of one of his drumsticks, thinking hard. "There's Mavis in the kitchen," he said, half joking. "She's always singing, isn't she?"

"Actually she's pretty good," said Tara. "I can't reach half the notes she can." She leaned over and gripped

Danny's arm. "Asking Mavis is a good idea," she said. "What if I got lots of staff involved? Why shouldn't everyone help if they want to? It would still be the students' midterm concert, but if we had extra people as well it would make it a little different and bring in more people to buy the CD." She let go of Danny's arm and got up.

"That might be an angle the local paper would like," she added, thinking of the publicity her mom had said she would need. "It would be the *whole* of Rockley Park working together to help the school in Africa. And if lots of people were appearing, they'd invite all *their* friends and relatives to watch, and just like Judge Jim said we could collect donations that night!"

"I saw Mr. Fallon going into a practice room with an Elvis tape last semester," Danny told Tara. "I wonder if he'd be interested in joining in?"

"Let's ask him!" said Tara. "And anyone else you can think of who might be good. They'll have to audition, of course. Perhaps Judge Jim would help with that. Meanwhile, I'll e-mail the local paper about it."

"I'll ask Mr. Fallon and the rest of the estate crew," offered Danny.

"I'll go to the admin office," Tara replied. "We can ask the kitchen staff at dinner. Don't be late!"

By dinnertime, Tara had discovered that one of the office staff played the guitar and a couple of others were in a choir in the town. She left them egging one another on, with the promise that they'd audition to perform something and ask all their friends to attend to help raise money for Nangila's school. It had helped that Tara had taken his photo there to be copied. All the staff remembered the picture of the little boy and were interested in his story. Tara had also been to see Mr. Timms, who'd agreed to record the concert for her charity CD. She arrived in the dining hall on a real high.

"Dave Fallon said *yes*!" Danny greeted her, grinning.

"What are you two up to?" asked Marmalade curiously.

"Hopefully, helping the African orphans," said Tara. "Everything's coming together now. I'm going to use the midterm concert as a fund-raiser, with some extra acts from the office and catering staff so we attract their friends and relatives, too. Mr. Timms is going to record it, and I'm going to sell the CDs afterward. It's going to be awesome!"

"Fantastic!" said Lolly. "That gets over the problem of Mr. Player not approving, too. He won't be able to complain that we're being distracted from chasing Rising Stars points now."

"Actually, I was hoping you might volunteer to design a poster," Tara said. "You and Pop are good at art and we'll need to put posters up in the town and send some to our parents as well."

Pop held up her hands. "Sorry, Tara," she said. "It's great that we can help out by singing now, but I'm not going to jeopardize Rising Stars points by taking on anything extra."

Tara sighed. It looked as if it was all up to her.

After dinner, Tara went straight for the computer in her dorm. She found the local newspaper's address and sent an e-mail to the editor, telling him all about Nangila and his school, and how Rockley Park proposed to help. She made a lot out of the fact that the staff would be performing alongside the students, hoping that the paper would pick up on this bit of local interest. She added that they were hoping as many people as possible would come. Then she pressed send, and the e-mail disappeared.

The next morning at break, everyone was buzzing excitedly about the midterm concert being turned into Tara's charity concert. All the students seemed to love the idea.

"We'll need a great finale," said Chloe. "Something to round it off so people are reminded why we want tons of donations."

"How about your song, Tara?" asked Ed.

"Good idea!" agreed Danny. "All the performers could come onstage and sing along to it at the end. That would be really cool!"

"Why don't we ask some people to come to the Rock Department after dinner for a quick tryout?" asked Pop.

"I thought you weren't supposed to be practicing anything except your song for the concert?" Tara pointed out sourly.

Pop blushed and Marmalade laughed. "I wondered where the old, grumpy Tara had gone," he said. Then it was Tara's turn to blush.

"Let's not fight," begged Lolly. "Tara deserves as much support as we can give her. If Mr. Player yells at us, that's just tough."

The day was going well, when Tara got a message from Mrs. Sharkey to go and see her after dinner.

As soon as she arrived at the principal's office, the secretary told Tara she could go right in. To her surprise, Mrs. Sharkey wasn't sitting behind her huge desk as usual. Instead, she was pacing up and down by the large window that overlooked the lake. Tara had never seen her so agitated.

As soon as Tara closed the door behind her, Mrs. Sharkey stopped pacing and turned to face her.

"Sit down," she said. Tara sat, feeling bewildered

and rather alarmed at Mrs. Sharkey's tone. "I've just received a phone call from the local paper."

Alarm bells began to ring. Was this something to do with the e-mail Tara had written? But it was a good e-mail. Tara had been almost certain it would get the publicity she needed.

Mrs. Sharkey sat down and glared at her. "I am informed by the editor that the school has invited the general public to a concert at Rockley Park in aid of a group of African orphans," she told Tara. "He tells me that it will be the more the merrier as far as the audience goes. Would you like to explain to me why the first I hear about these arrangements is in a phone call from a newspaper?"

Tara gulped. It hadn't occurred to her to show Mrs. Sharkey the e-mail before she'd sent it. But Mrs. Sharkey was waiting for an explanation and Tara would have to say something. "It is for *charity*," she said in a small voice.

"Your reasons are not in question," Mrs. Sharkey said coldly. "But you should *never* send e-mails to newspapers before clearing them with me. Apart from it being extremely rude to keep me in the dark about your plans, it is not up to *you* to decide who is invited onto school property."

She rose to her feet and resumed her pacing.

"I told the editor that he had his facts wrong," she told Tara. "And I apologized for wasting his time. We are a small, independent school. Even if we wanted to invite outsiders to our concerts, we could not do so. We don't have anything like a large enough theater. You know very well that there are very few spare seats when the parents come to concerts."

She stopped and glared at Tara again.

"The editor seemed to have some idea that we would be *selling* tickets," she went on. "Did you tell him that?"

Tara shook her head. "No," she said quietly.

Mrs. Sharkey folded her arms. "He also had the extraordinary idea that the catering and admin staff would be *doing turns*, as he put it. Utter nonsense. What sort of school do you think I am running? The midterm concert is an important educational tool, not a free-for-all!"

Tara shrank in her chair from the blazing anger in the principal's face. "Whatever you may think," Mrs. Sharkey told her, "you are *not* in charge of this school. Although you will no doubt be pleased to hear that the orphans' charity *will* be supported in some way by Rockley Park, it will be done in a proper manner, at a later date, without you riding roughshod over every correct procedure. That will be all."

She went to the door and held it open. Tara wanted to protest, but she knew it would do no good. It wouldn't help if she tried to explain that she hadn't thought she was doing anything wrong. It hadn't occurred to her that the theater was too small, or that the editor would call the school about her e-mail, or even that Mrs. Sharkey would be angry if he did.

She got up and left the room. The door closed behind her with a firm click. It was the end of everything. She'd let everyone down—mostly, of course, the children she was trying to help, but also all the people at school who were looking forward to being part of the fund-raiser. Now she would have to tell them that it wasn't going to happen.

How could she possibly face her friends in the Rock Department? They would all be there, waiting for her to arrive so they could practice her song. For once, Tara's strength of character deserted her. She knew she should give them the bad news right away, but she just couldn't.

Instead, she went over to Paddock House and up to her bedroom. The room was empty. On the wall above Tara's bed was the blown-up photograph of Nangila with Lolly. Tara looked up into his frightened eyes. For the first time in years, she could do nothing to stop the tears. She sank down onto her bed and began to cry.

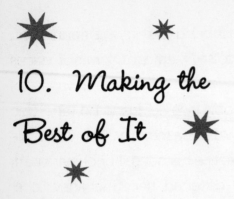

10. Making the Best of It

After a while, Tara fumbled for a tissue and blew her nose. She wiped her eyes and sniffed. This was getting her nowhere. What if someone came into the room? She couldn't let anyone see her like this. Tara Fitzgerald never cried.

She blew her nose again and went into the bathroom. She washed her face with cold water to try to get rid of the telltale red marks around her eyes.

You have to go and tell them, she told herself fiercely. *Hurry up, before they all leave the rehearsal. You have to let them know what happened.*

It was the last thing in the world she wanted to do, but before she could talk herself out of it, she walked firmly downstairs and over toward the Rock Department.

As she opened the door a great chorus of voices met her, lifted in song. The large main room was full of people singing her words, while Danny, Ed, and Ben played. Judge Jim was standing in for Tara. He gestured for her to take over, but Tara shook her head. She had managed to make herself come here, but no way did she feel able to perform.

She stood numbly and listened until they'd finished. They were all enjoying themselves so much, and the song sounded fantastic, but it was all for nothing.

As the last notes faded, Tara ventured farther into the room. Judge Jim put down his guitar and smiled at her before disappearing into his office.

"You've been gone *forever*!" yelled Pop. "And we've been having such a great time!"

"Did you like your song?" asked Chloe. "It sounds wonderful with us all singing, doesn't it?"

Tara nodded. "Yes," she told them all, forcing her voice to be strong. "It does sound good...but I'm afraid I've got some bad news." In spite of all her efforts, her voice was wobbling badly, but no one seemed to notice.

"Oh no! What?" asked Ben. "Don't say you want to change the song. It's perfect just as it is."

"It's my fault," Tara continued. "I've annoyed Mrs. Sharkey, and now she's not going to let anyone other than students perform. And she said the concert should be educational, not a free-for-all, so I guess the finale is off, too."

Everyone started talking at once.

"She can't do that!"

"That's not fair!"

"What about this song? We *have* to sing it!"

"Mrs. Sharkey did say that Rockley Park will help support Nangila's school in the future, but not yet and not using my plan."

"Well, at least the charity won't suffer," said Lolly, smiling at Tara encouragingly.

"And this is still a great song," chipped in Ed. "I bet we'll be able to use it in the future, Tara. Come on, cheer up."

"That's right," said Ben, picking up the melody of the verse again. "Don't let old Sharkey spoil everything. Let's play your song again."

"I've got to go," said Tara. "Sorry. But keep going."

"See you later," called Lolly.

Tara made her way back out of the building. They were all on a high in there. But Tara felt bitterly sad and let down by her own behavior. She hadn't meant to annoy Mrs. Sharkey. She had only tried to help as many children as possible. She couldn't bear to think that she'd made things worse instead of better.

It was small consolation that the school was going to adopt the charity. Mrs. Sharkey didn't seem to have any sense of urgency about it. It could be weeks or months before any fund-raising ideas were tried out. What would happen to Nangila in the meantime?

A little while later Tara's roommates came back, chatting excitedly.

"That was *so much* fun!" exclaimed Chloe, sinking onto her bed with a sigh of satisfaction. "I'm sorry things didn't work out, though, Tara. At least the charity will still get some help."

"Are you all right?" Lolly added.

"Of course," replied Tara quickly.

"What did you do to upset Mrs. Sharkey so much?" asked Pop curiously.

Tara looked at her resentfully. She had hoped that no one would ask that.

"She didn't like that I tried to get publicity for the concert," she muttered.

"Oh, Tara," said Lolly, sounding so sympathetic that Tara was afraid she might burst into tears again. "That's such a shame. And you were only trying to help the children."

Tara swallowed hard and forced herself to look unmoved.

"Well, I failed," she managed, before she had to turn away. She picked up a book and tried to read, but the page blurred, and she couldn't make out a single word.

It was almost seven o'clock when Mrs. Pinto put her head around the door.

"Is it homework time already?" asked Chloe, looking at her watch.

"You've got a few minutes yet," Mrs. Pinto told her. "No, it's Tara I was looking for. Tara, Mrs. Sharkey would like to see you right away."

Tara stood up. It was very late in the day to be seeing the principal. Something must be terribly wrong. Was it more fallout from her e-mail to the newspaper or was it worse than that? Could it be something to do with her parents? Had there been an accident?

Tara was in agony as she sprinted over to the main house. "Please let Mom and Dad be all right," she muttered over and over again as she climbed the stairs up to the principal's office.

The door to Mrs. Sharkey's room was open, and the secretary waved her right in. But Tara could hear voices in there. The principal wasn't alone. It *must* have something to do with her parents, and someone had come to give her the awful news. But the secretary didn't notice how frightened Tara was.

"Go on," she urged impatiently from where she sat at her desk. "Don't keep them waiting."

Tara took a deep breath and pushed the door open. With Mrs. Sharkey was Judge Jim and a man Tara had never seen before. He was wearing a dark suit, and looked like a businessman of some sort.

"Ah! Come in, Tara," said Mrs. Sharkey. "We've been waiting for you."

Judge Jim patted an empty chair next to him and gave Tara a kind smile. She glanced at the strange man for a moment and then did as she was told.

Judge Jim pushed a small plate and a napkin toward her, and Tara realized that she had interrupted *something*. A large platter of dainty sandwiches was in the middle of the desk, along with a couple of bowls of chips and nuts. It didn't look like bad news if the kitchen had been asked to send sandwiches up. What on earth was going on?

"This is Mr. Boyd," Mrs. Sharkey told her.

Mr. Boyd held out his hand, and as Tara shook it, she realized who he was. Mr. Boyd was the editor of the *Daily News*, the newspaper she'd written to about the concert. What was he doing in the principal's office? She found it impossible to read his expression.

"More wine?" offered Mrs. Sharkey. "Or would you rather have coffee?" Judge Jim was already on his feet, waiting to refill Mr. Boyd's glass. "There's orange juice," she told Tara, "or coffee if you'd prefer it."

"Orange, please," said Tara faintly. It seemed she was being invited to join some sort of party. Judge Jim passed her a large glass of freshly squeezed orange juice.

Everyone except Tara looked very pleased with themselves, but Tara, nibbling on a chip, was still very much in the dark. Was she in trouble or wasn't she? None of this made any sense. But at last Mrs. Sharkey took pity on her.

"I expect poor Tara is wondering what all this is about," she said, taking a sip of coffee and setting the cup down. "I have to tell you that she and I were not on the best of terms after she went over my head by e-mailing you, Mr. Boyd."

Mr. Boyd, who was much younger than Tara had imagined the editor to be, nodded understandingly.

"I'm sorry we all got off to a bad start," he agreed.

Mrs. Sharkey smiled at Tara. She looked encouraging.

"Mr. Boyd has come here this evening because he has a proposal for us," she told Tara. "And his proposal involves you."

Mr. Boyd cleared his throat and smiled at Tara.

"I was so impressed with your e-mail," he told her. "I thought such enterprise needed supporting, and I approached Mrs. Sharkey to see if we could help. I hadn't realized then that your theater couldn't accommodate more than a few hundred people, or that you hadn't asked her permission to open the school concert to the public."

Tara blushed.

"After I spoke to your principal, I realized that if we were going to make the most of your excellent idea, you needed much more help than I'd first thought!"

Tara returned his smile warily. Where on earth was this going?

"Our parent company," he said, "the one that owns my newspaper, has a history of supporting events throughout the country. I called the publicity department, and they told me that the outdoor stage is free for one weekend next month." He looked at Tara as if he expected her to be thrilled. "There's been a cancellation," he added, as if that explained everything.

Tara looked at Judge Jim for help. She had no idea what the editor was talking about.

"Mr. Boyd has offered Mrs. Sharkey his company's portable open-air stage for the midterm concert so we can entertain many more people," he told her gently. "And Mrs. Sharkey has accepted."

Mrs. Sharkey was nodding encouragingly.

"We couldn't turn down such a generous offer," she said. "Of course, we will have to apply to the council for a license, and we have to consider things like parking and road access. But Mr. Fallon is hopeful that he can put everything in place in time."

"I was very attracted to your idea of including everyone—staff and students," said Mr. Boyd. "I love the way Rockley Park is like one big family, with everyone eager to help."

Tara glanced at Mrs. Sharkey. The principal was looking at her sternly now, so Tara looked away.

"Mr. Fallon thinks that if we use the large field at the back of Rockley Park House, the capacity will be about two thousand," Judge Jim said. Tara gasped. Two thousand people! She had never dreamed that the concert could possibly attract so many.

"I have never wanted to expose our students prematurely to the public eye," Mrs. Sharkey told Tara. "But Judge Jim assures me that the experience of performing on a large, outdoor stage is too good to miss. The students are already rehearsing hard for the midterm concert, and I know they'll give their best, for the sake of Rising Stars points *and* your charity, Tara." She looked at her with steely eyes. "This doesn't mean that I'm going to adopt *every* scheme you throw at me," she added. Tara nodded meekly.

"Mr. Timms has already agreed to record the concert, hasn't he?" said Judge Jim, smiling at Tara.

"And you'll be able to sell copies of the CD afterward."

Tara nodded and managed a small smile. First the fund-raising was on, then it was off, and now it was on again. Earlier today she'd thought that she'd really blown it, but it seemed everything was going to be all right after all.

Judge Jim and the others were all looking at her, waiting for her to say something, but for once Tara was totally at a loss for words. She managed another small smile, and the adults laughed.

"I think she likes the idea," said Mr. Boyd.

11. Concert Fever

From that moment, the days flew by. One of the jobs was to mark out a stage-size area for the students to practice on. Judge Jim, with Tara and some others to help, paced it out on the front lawn.

"It's important to be able to rehearse in the right-size space," Judge Jim told them. "If you don't, you'll look lost when you get up on that open-air stage."

"But it's *huge*!" said Ben, looking distinctly worried.

"You have to learn to take charge of the space," Judge Jim said as he unwound and pegged down a long strip of white tape while they stood, one at each corner. "Come into the middle now, and stand how you usually do when you're playin' as a band."

There seemed to be acres of space to spare within the tape.

"Look how big an area you'll have to move around in," he showed them. "Pretend you're playin' your song, but use the space. Make it yours. Don't let it intimidate you."

It was scary to begin with, but they soon got the hang of it. They moved farther apart, and decided to take turns stepping forward, right to the edge of the stage, to play a few solo bars.

"It's not fair!" Danny called out from where he was sitting in the center of the marked-out rectangle. "I'm the only one who has to stay put."

"You need your drums on wheels." Ed laughed.

"At least you'll be on a raised platform so everyone can see you," Judge Jim told him with a smile. "As soon as the stage is set up, everyone will get a chance to do a live run-through, but for the next few days, each performer can use this space to visualize how they'll behave on the real stage."

The practice space was very popular, but everyone

was really looking forward to the real stage arriving. Meanwhile, all the students were very busy, but Tara was exhausted. Not only was she going to her ordinary classes, and trying to find time to rehearse her song with Danny and the others, but the organization of the charity concert was taking every other spare waking minute.

She was the one everyone went to when they wanted questions to be answered, and if Tara didn't have the answer she had to find it. She had organized the art department to make flyers, and had been given permission by Mrs. Sharkey for them to be mailed to all the parents. She had even gotten the name and address of Tikki Deacon's agent from Pop and Lolly so she could invite Tikki to the concert.

"I know she won't come," Tara told Pop as she sealed the envelope and put it in her bag to mail later, "but I might as well invite her."

Pop giggled. "You have such nerve, Tara. I don't know how you do it."

Tara lay back on the grass, snatching a few precious moments of relaxation in the sun.

"You never know," said Lolly thoughtfully. "Tikki might show up. After all, it's her pet charity."

Pop shook her head. "She's abroad so much," she reminded her sister. "She probably won't even get the invitation in time."

Tara shrugged. "Like my parents," she said gruffly. "Their flyer will probably still be in the envelope when I go home for summer vacation."

Chloe looked shocked. "I admire you, Tara," she said. "I'd be so upset if my parents didn't show up. And you've done *so* much for this event. It's just not fair."

"Well, *we* all appreciate it," Lolly told Tara. "And Nangila and his friends will, too. That's what matters."

Tara didn't reply. She was trying very hard not to think about her parents too much. She had called her dad a few days earlier, but he'd been sort of noncommittal about whether he'd be able to make it to the concert. Well, Tara wouldn't beg. But this was *her* project, and everyone else's families were coming. In the middle of so much excitement, Tara was feeling very let down.

"What's going on?" demanded Pop, staring hard across the grass.

Several large trucks had pulled up outside the main house and one of the drivers was getting out.

"I think it must be the stage," replied Tara, getting up and heading toward the trucks. She was right. Dave Fallon arrived to give the driver directions and all the trucks drove slowly around to the back field and started to unload. There seemed to be thousands of scaffolding poles, plus yards and yards of colorful fabric.

"How are they ever going to make that into a stage?" asked Chloe, staring in confusion as piles of equipment were unloaded onto the grass.

It took a while, but by the end of the day there was a recognizable platform, and by the afternoon of the second day the huge canopy was up, protecting the stage from any threat of rain. Now swarms of men were setting up the lighting and the sound systems. Cables and equipment were everywhere.

With all the excitement, it was hard to concentrate

on normal classes. But in art one afternoon there was a treat in store for Tara and her friends.

"I thought you might like to see the CD inserts we've had printed," the art teacher said. "And the CD cases have arrived. If you like, you can put some inserts in the cases today."

Tara felt really choked up as she put the first insert into a plastic CD case. The art department had done a great job. On the front, Nangila looked out with his lonely, frightened eyes. He'd been given a colorful background of reds and yellows, suggesting the heat of Africa. *Singing for Nangila* was printed along the bottom in black lettering. On the inside, Tara had written a bit about the charity and the school, with help from Pop and Lolly.

Judge Jim had advised Tara about acknowledgments, and so Tara had made sure there was space on the back for thanking Mrs. Sharkey, Mr. Timms, Mr. Boyd and his newspaper, and everyone else who was involved. She turned the CD case over to read it and got a big surprise. Right at the bottom, in tiny letters, it said:

Special thanks to Tara Fitzgerald, without whom this CD would never have happened. Tara's face glowed.

Pop was grinning at her. "We asked the art department to put that on after you'd seen the proofs," she told her triumphantly. "We wanted it to be a surprise."

"But the CD *hasn't* really happened yet," Tara reminded her.

Pop and Lolly both laughed. "There have been some ups and downs," Lolly said. "But nothing is going to stop it now. Look, even Mrs. Sharkey has added a note."

I am pleased to launch our new relationship with Nangila's school by endorsing this live CD of the midterm concert held at Rockley Park School, Tara read. She felt very humble. Her hopes and dreams were actually going to come true.

The stage was out-of-bounds to students until the technicians had finished their work, but in spite of that, the following evening Tara was asked to meet Judge Jim there. As she went into the field and got close to the stage for the first time, she could see just how big the structure was. She felt dwarfed by it. As she looked, a bank of lights came on in the shade of the canopy. They changed from red to blue to white and orange. Then they went off again. The technicians were still busy. Out in front of the stage another bank of spotlights was fixed to a scaffolding tower. Inside the tower at ground level was Mr. Timms's equipment, a miniversion of his mixing desk in the recording studio, connected to all the onstage amps and microphones. He would be in charge of all the sound on the day, as well as recording the concert for Tara's CD.

The grass had been crushed by all the activity, and was now turning pale yellow. It smelled warmly of hay. Around the back of the stage there were cables everywhere, and a generator was running. Tara found some steps and climbed up to the backstage area.

Judge Jim was there, talking to one of the technicians. "What do you think?" he asked Tara with a smile. "Go on, see how it feels."

Tara walked out onto the stage, and stopped. She had been on stages before, but this was different. She could feel the breeze on her face, and hear a car passing on the road and the noise of the generator below. And the space in front of her seemed to go on forever, with the dusk blurring the edges of the field. It was totally different from being on a stage indoors. And this stage was so high. It was going to be hard to feel in charge up here, in spite of Judge Jim's marked-out practice rectangle. She was happy that she would be playing in a band, not singing on her own.

"None of this would have happened without you," Judge Jim told her quietly. "You've done really well, Tara. You should be proud of yourself."

Tara felt more awestruck than proud. What had started out as a big idea had grown into a real event, and it had been emotionally and physically exhausting getting there.

Judge Jim left her alone with her thoughts for a moment while he went backstage. When he came back he was carrying something. "Thought you might want this," he said. "I brought it over for you." Tara turned and saw that he held her beloved Rickenbacker bass. "How about tryin' the sound?" he suggested.

Tara's face lit up.

Judge Jim showed her which amp to plug into and then picked up his own, battered old guitar.

There was a sort of magic in the air. After all the hard work, Tara was more tired than she had ever been before, but with the Rickenbacker in her hands she felt new energy flooding through her. She was onstage with the legendary Judge Jim Henson and anything was possible. He nodded at her encouragingly and she started the intro to her song.

There were no drums or rhythm guitar and the sound was thin, with no microphones to boost their voices, but Tara soon lost herself in the emotion of the song. Halfway through, the lights came on again, bathing them both in red and blue tones. Tara almost lost her place, but as the beams cut through the dusk and flooded them with color she recovered, and as the final notes of their duet died away she turned to Judge Jim, her heart full and her eyes glistening with tears. Now, at this moment, it seemed entirely possible that she might make the money she wanted for Nangila after all.

"Thought you might like to be the first to play up here," Judge Jim told her gently when she thanked him. "Go on, then," he added. "I'll take your bass back. You get on back to your dorm. I think you could benefit from an early night. It's goin' to be another long day tomorrow."

12. Lonely Eyes

After another couple of frantic days putting the final touches in place, the concert date finally arrived. By the middle of the afternoon, the field was filling up. Lots of people had brought picnics. Blankets, chairs, and picnic tables were dotted around everywhere as the large crowd settled down to enjoy themselves.

But there was no relaxation for Tara, and after she'd gotten everyone through their sound checks, her voice was beginning to sound rather hoarse.

"It's all the bossing around you've done," Ben told her.

"But I *had* to," Tara objected. "Otherwise we'd still be sound-checking now!"

"I know," Danny said soothingly. "But you don't need to talk anymore. Would a cough drop help?"

"No!" said Chloe. "That isn't what you should do. Mr. Player always says it's best to rest your voice as much as possible, and drink honey, lemon, and ginger."

"I'll go and get you some from the sickbay," Pop offered. "Sister O'Flannery is really good at making it."

"Keep your throat warm, too," advised Lolly. "Here, take this." She unwound a long silk scarf from her neck and arranged it around Tara's. "Don't say anything!" she added as Tara was about to thank her. "Save your voice for later."

Hanging around between the sound check in the morning and the beginning of the concert that afternoon was the hardest part. "Don't start thinking about *rain*," Tara begged Danny, when he told her a large black cloud was approaching. "You'll give *everyone* the jitters."

"Stop *talking*," begged Ben. "We're going to need your voice later."

Thankfully, the day stayed sunny, even though the breeze was a little chilly.

As the time for the concert approached, the audience packed away their picnics and moved closer to the stage. Then the lights came on, and Mrs. Sharkey appeared onstage to welcome everyone.

Tara hardly listened to the short speech. She was too busy making sure the performers were all in place and ready to play their parts.

As soon as Mrs. Sharkey came off, Judge Jim went on to announce the first act. He was greeted with enthusiastic applause.

"Go ahead," Tara said quietly to Charlie Owen and his band, who were waiting for their cue. She gave them a shove and they ran out onto the stage to a rousing cheer.

"The audience is determined to enjoy itself," Judge Jim told her as he joined Tara at the side of the stage. "It's the best sort of audience you could possibly have. They'd cheer a cabbage if you put one on!"

That made Tara laugh, and most of her anxiety about the concert melted away.

One by one, the performers gave their best. Chloe's

awesome voice stilled the crowd, and Pop and Lolly got a huge reception because they were so famous. The staff band Judge Jim had put together was a real treat for the students, and Mr. Fallon's excellent performance got a resounding cheer. From the staff to the students, the newspaper people, and the audience, everyone was entering into the spirit of the day. The people here at Rockley Park, Tara told herself, were the only family she needed.

There were also Rising Stars points to be earned. All the students knew the teachers were watching every move and assessing every note. The novelty of the open-air stage brought extra excitement to the event, and the huge audience was lifting the students to even greater efforts.

Tara was glad she wasn't competing for Rising Stars points. She would simply play her song as best she could, and not worry about it too much. It was more important for her to keep the concert going without a hitch.

All too soon the finale was drawing near. Danny, Ed,

and Ben were waiting with Tara as Judge Jim went out to introduce the final act. Tara took a last sip of water, Ben handed her the Rickenbacker bass, and then they were on!

They were picked out in the glow of blue and green spotlights, and now that she was onstage Tara realized she *did* care about her performance after all.

After the crowd had clapped them on, it fell quiet. Tara didn't know what Judge Jim had said when he introduced them—she had been too wound up to listen—but it must have been something serious about their special song.

She glanced at her band. Danny was all set behind his drum kit, and Ed and Ben were plugged in and ready to go. Tara gave them a nod, and walked right out to the front of the stage, a small, determined figure. Then she began to play.

The sonorous tones of her Rickenbacker rang out over the crowd. She played the intro a little faster than they'd rehearsed it, with her head hung low over the frets. Nervousness was speeding her fingers, but it sounded good, and her band was right with her. Her voice hadn't quite gone, but it was cracking as she brought her head up to sing the first verse, and Ed came over and joined her at the microphone to help her get the words out. They were rocking hard and fast, the melody ripping along to Danny's heavy beat.

Then Tara and Ed stepped back as Ben took over, the high wail of his guitar changing the mood.

Tara was grateful when Ed joined her at the microphone again for the second verse. She was belting out the words, but hardly anything was left of her voice. Ben played the middle eight bars as a solo, and then Ed and Tara came in again to repeat the hook and sing the last verse. All the while, Danny was keeping them in time, his thumping beat pushing the music on.

Then it was over, and they bowed together, soaking up the applause. Tara looked around for Judge Jim, and after a moment he came and joined them. The crowd was already calling for more from Tara's band, but he held up his arms and managed to calm them down.

"I just want to say a couple of things," he said into Tara's microphone, adjusting it upward as he did so. "None of this would have happened if it wasn't for this young lady here. So let's hear it for Tara Fitzgerald!" The crowd roared, louder than it had all through the concert, and Judge Jim grinned at her. "Do you want to say something?" he asked quietly.

Tara shook her head. "I've lost my voice," she croaked, holding the scarf to her throat. It was true. Her voice had finally given out.

"She's lost her voice, unfortunately," Judge Jim told the crowd. There was some laughter, and then the crowd burst into applause again. "Well, I'm sure Tara would thank you all for coming, if she could speak," the Head of Rock confirmed. "And for supportin' her wonderful effort at raisin' money for the orphaned children of Africa." There was thunderous applause again, and Judge Jim had to wait until it subsided.

"In a moment," he said, "we're goin' to get everyone onstage to sing 'Lonely Eyes' again, but before we do, I think we have somethin'..." He looked to the side of the stage, and on came Mr. Boyd with a huge bouquet of flowers. He gave them to Tara and waved at the crowd before walking off.

"We're most grateful to our sponsors," Judge Jim added. "Without the *Daily News*, this would have been impossible to stage. Now, we don't want those lovely flowers squashed when everyone comes up here. D'you want to put them somewhere safe, Tara? No..." he added as she made to go backstage. "Take them off to the right. Someone can take them from you..."

Tara looked to where he was pointing, but the lights were in her eyes and she couldn't see much. Judge Jim was talking to the audience again as Tara carried her bouquet to the side of the stage. The perfume was wonderful in the dusk. Tara couldn't stop looking at the flowers. She buried her face in the cool petals for a moment, drinking in the scent. It reminded her of some of the wonderful flowers she'd seen in Africa, and that made her think of Nangila. She'd never met him, but she'd thought about him so often she felt she knew him. Well, his concert was almost over, and it had been a real success. Maybe there would be enough money to make a difference in his life.

As she came offstage, a couple of people held out their hands. Tara went to put the bouquet into them, and then stopped. For a moment, her heart faltered. She couldn't believe what she was seeing.

It was Mom . . . and Dad. They were smiling at her, and her mom had tears in her eyes.

"We're *so* proud of you," said Tara's mom, putting the flowers down and giving her daughter a huge hug.

"What an amazing song!" said her dad, hugging her, too. "We managed to rearrange our schedules and decided to surprise you. I'm so glad we did. We're so, so proud of you!"

Maybe it was just as well that Tara had lost her voice. She couldn't have spoken even if she'd wanted to, she was so choked up.

"Hurry. You're needed back onstage," said Pop, who'd been sent to find Tara.

"Oh yes!" said Tara's dad. "They're going to do your

song again with all the performers. They can't do it without you!"

"Come with me," Tara begged. But they couldn't hear her whispered words. "Please," she mouthed, tugging at their hands. Then Tara mimed the saxophone and her mom laughed.

"You know him," she said. "He never goes anywhere without it. Anyway, Judge Jim told him to be sure to bring it today, just in case."

Tara gave her dad a push. "Go and get it," she whispered. "Play with me. Please. You never, ever have."

"All right," he agreed, understanding at last. "If you're sure. It's your day."

The stage was getting crowded. And they were all waiting for Tara. As she appeared with her parents, Chloe began to clap. The rest of the students joined in, and as Tara came farther onstage, everyone, performers and audience alike, applauded.

Somehow she made it to her Rickenbacker. She put the strap over her head. As her shoulder took the familiar, reassuring weight, she glanced at her parents.

Her mom was smiling, and her dad was moistening the mouthpiece of his sax. He caught Tara's eye and winked.

"Let's rock," he mouthed, grinning.

Tara gave him a nod, and walked right out to the very front of the stage.

Then she began to play.

So you want to be a pop star?

Turn the page to read some top tips on how to make your dreams come true....

✳ *Making it in the music biz* ✳

Think you've got tons of talent?
Well, music maestro Judge Jim Henson,
Head of Rock at talent academy Rockley Park,
has put together his top tips to help
you become a superstar....

✳ Number One Rule: Be positive!
You've got to believe in yourself.

✳ Be active! Join your school choir
or form your own band.

✳ Be different! Don't be afraid to stand
out from the crowd.

✳ Be determined! Work hard and stay focused.

✳ Be creative! Try writing your own material—
it will say something unique about you.

✳ Be patient! Don't give up if things
don't happen overnight.

✳ Be ready to seize opportunities
when they come along.

✳ Be versatile! Don't have a one-track mind—try out new things and gain as many skills as you can.

✳ Be passionate! Don't be afraid to show some emotion in your performance.

✳ Be sure to watch, listen, and learn all the time.

✳ Be willing to help others. You'll learn more that way.

✳ Be smart! Don't neglect your schoolwork.

✳ Be cool and don't get bigheaded! Everyone needs friends, so don't leave them behind.

✳ Always stay true to yourself.

✳ And finally, and most important, enjoy what you do!

✳ *Go for it! It's all up to you now....*

CINDY JEFFERIES's varied career has included being a Venetian-mask maker and a video DJ. Cindy decided to write *Fame School* after experiencing the ups and downs of her children, who have all been involved in the music business. Her insight into the lives of wannabe pop stars and her own musical background means that Cindy knows how exciting and demanding the quest for fame and fortune can be.

Cindy lives on a farm in Gloucestershire, England, where the animal noises, roaring tractors, and rehearsals of Stitch, her son's indie-rock band, all help her write!

To find out more about Cindy Jefferies, visit her Web site: www.cindyjefferies.co.uk